M. Longden

KU-476-743

Dinosaurs lived on Earth millions of years ago. Their name means ''terrible lizard'' and although no one has ever seen a living dinosaur we know a lot about them because fossil dinosaur bones have been found all over the world. This book describes a large number of these exciting creatures, including the gentle, plant-eating Diplodocus and the fierce, meat-eating Tyrannosaurus. It also looks at the frightening array of teeth, claws and armour that dinosaurs used for hunting and protection.

Acknowledgments:
The publishers would like to thank Wendy Body for acting as reading level consultant and the British Museum of Natural History for advising on scientific content.

Photographic credits:
Pages 36 and 39, G. S. F. Picture Library; pages 40 and 41 bottom, The Mansell Collection; page 41 top, Ann Ronan Picture Library; page 43, The British Museum of Natural History.

British Library Cataloguing in Publication Data
Daly, Bridget
    Dinosaurs.
    1. Dinosaurs
    I. Title   II. Woods, Michael   III. Forsey, Chris
    567.9'1
    ISBN 0-7214-1107-X

First edition
Published by Ladybird Books Ltd Loughborough Leicestershire UK
Ladybird Books Inc Auburn Maine 04210 USA

Printed in England

Dinosaurs

written by BRIDGET DALY
and MICHAEL WOODS

illustrated by CHRIS FORSEY

Ladybird Books

What were the dinosaurs?

Millions of years ago, long before there were people on Earth, huge monsters roamed our planet. They were *reptiles*, like crocodiles and lizards. Some of these reptiles swam in the sea or flew in the air. But one special kind, the *dinosaurs*, were lords of the land. They lasted for 160 million years.

The word "dinosaur" was invented by the English scientist Richard Owen in 1841. It means "terrible lizard" in Greek.

There were many different kinds of dinosaurs. Some were giant, peaceful plant-eaters…

…and some dinosaurs had deadly slashing teeth and claws which they used to kill and eat other reptiles.

The age of dinosaurs

The world looked quite different when dinosaurs first appeared

Development of animals time chart

Number of years ago

4,600 million
Earth formed

3,800 million
First living things

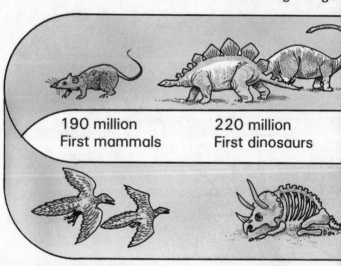

190 million
First mammals

220 million
First dinosaurs

145 million
First birds

65 million
Dinosaurs die out

on Earth, about 220 million years ago. There were no buildings and no roads and no humans. The weather was very warm all the year round.

| 500 million | 400 million | 380 million |
| First fish | First land plants | First insects |

| 300 million | 345 million |
| First reptiles | First amphibians |

| 55 million | 2 million | Present |
| Age of mammals | First humans | day |

Dinosaur ancestors

The first ancestors of the dinosaurs were fish called *lobefins*. They began to pull themselves out of the water onto the land. Gradually over millions of years the first

Eusthenopteron was a lobefin about 1 m long. It was a fierce, bony freshwater fish. It had strong muscles in its fins to support it on land. It had lungs as well as gills so it could breathe air out of water for short periods.

amphibians appeared. They were halfway between a fish and a land animal, like the frogs, toads and newts of today. Amphibians could live part of the time on land.

Ichthyostega was one of the first amphibians. It had lungs and proper legs and feet. But it had to return to water to keep its skin wet and to lay its eggs.

From amphibians to reptiles

Amphibians could live on dry land but they had to stay near water. Slowly, over millions of years, some kinds of amphibians developed into reptiles. Reptiles could live on land all the time. They had scaly waterproof skins to stop them drying out and their eggs had tough shells to protect them.

Seymouria

The secret of the reptiles' success was their eggs. Amphibians' eggs are small and soft, like frogspawn. They dry up and die if they are left out of water.

Reptiles' eggs have a tough waterproof shell which does not dry out. Safe inside the shell the young reptile is fed with a large supply of yolk until it hatches out.

Hylonomus

It is difficult to tell the difference between this small early reptile, **Hylonomus**, and this amphibian, **Seymouria**. But Hylonomus had a drier scaly skin to protect it from damage and the drying sun and wind.

The first dinosaurs

Dinosaurs probably developed from a type of reptile called *thecodonts,* which were something like our crocodiles. Dinosaurs held their legs under their bodies. Some could run fast on their back legs using their tails to balance. Other large heavy creatures walked on two or four legs.

Coelophysis was a light and speedy meat-eating dinosaur. It had clawed "hands" and many small sharp teeth. It is seen here with a small plant-eating dinosaur called **Heterodontosaurus**.

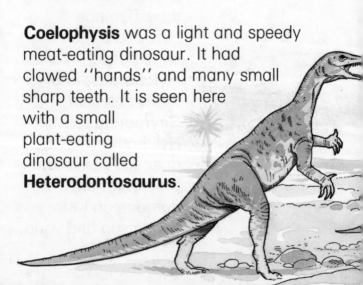

Reptiles such as lizards waddle along on bent sprawling legs.

Thecodonts held their legs more under their bodies.

Dinosaurs' legs were tucked well under their bodies, supporting their weight. This meant they could stand taller and run faster.

All shapes and sizes

Scientists have discovered over 800 species of dinosaurs. Over the millions of years that they roamed Earth, dinosaurs came in many weird and wonderful shapes and sizes. **Mamenchisaurus** was as long as four buses parked in a row but **Compsognathus** was no bigger than a chicken.

Compsognathus was 60 cm long and a fast-running meat-eater.

Stegosaurus was 7 m long but had a brain the size of a walnut.

The largest dinosaur footprints ever found were so big that they could hold as much water as a bath. They were found in Texas, USA.

Triceratops was 9 m long. Its fearsome horns measured 1 m.

Mamenchisaurus was 22 m long, 4 m high and weighed about 30 tonnes.

Gentle giants

The largest dinosaurs were called *sauropods*. They had huge bodies, long necks and even longer tails. But they were very slow and had tiny brains. They could feed only on soft plants as their teeth were weak and stumpy. They needed to eat a huge amount to keep themselves alive and had enormous stomachs.

Diplodocus was the longest land animal ever known. Its neck was 8 m long, its body 5 m and its tail a massive 14 m.

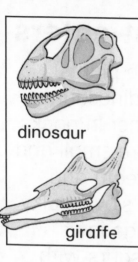

dinosaur

giraffe

This dinosaur skull shows that plant-eating dinosaurs had small even teeth, rather like this giraffe's front teeth. They were used for stripping leaves off plants.

Brachiosaurus

Diplodocus

Eating the highest leaves is **Brachiosaurus**. It weighed 80 tonnes, more than fifteen elephants. Its very long front legs gave it extra height.

17

Monster meat-eaters

Not all dinosaurs ate plants.
Many fed on other dinosaurs.
Some hunted together in packs
or groups. They were small and
fast, with slashing teeth and
claws. Others were slow, bulky
monsters whose huge jaws
could bite into dinosaurs with
thick, tough skins.

Deinonychus
was the fiercest,
fastest flesh-eater. It slashed
its prey with its huge razor-sharp
second claw which was 12 cm long.

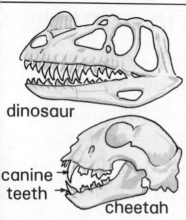

dinosaur

canine teeth →

cheetah

The skull of a meat-eating dinosaur had long sharp teeth like steak knives for tearing flesh. See how the shape of the teeth are quite like the canine teeth of a cheetah.

Megalosaurus was the first dinosaur to be given a name. It weighed 9 tonnes. Like many large meat-eaters it had a round bulky shape.

Dinosaurs in armour

The big slow plant-eaters could not easily get away from their enemies. Some of them, called *ankylosaurs*, had heavy bony plates and spines over their backs and tails. These protected them from attack, like a suit of armour.

The back of **Euoplocephalus** was completely covered with bony lumps and spikes in a leathery skin. Its head had a "helmet" of hard plates. Even its eyelids had bony coverings.

Paleoscincus had a heavy body and short legs. A fringe of sharp spikes stuck out all round the edge of its armour.

Polacanthus had a bony shield on its hips and a double row of spines on its neck and back.

A herd of three-horned **Triceratops**
surrounds an attacking **Tyrannosaurus**.
Even a fierce killer like this would
probably have run away when faced
with those horns.

Great defenders

Some dinosaurs looked rather like our modern rhinos. They had terrifying horns to defend themselves and a bony neck frill for protection. They were all plant-eaters and their enormously strong jaws must have tackled very tough food.

Protoceratops was a small, horned dinosaur. It was one of the first of this group and had only bony lumps, not true horns.

Lumps, bumps and crests

The oddest shaped heads in the dinosaur kingdom belonged to duckbilled dinosaurs called *hadrosaurs*. Their lumps, bumps and crests were mostly hollow and joined to the air-holes in their noses. But no one knows what they were for, although there are several ideas.

Parasaurolophus had a crest 2 m long, the size of a man! Perhaps it was used to push aside undergrowth as the animal moved along.

Tsintaosaurus had a hollow horn on its forehead which may have been used like a trumpet.

Pachycephalosaurus was not a hadrosaur but it also had a strange head. The dome on top was about 25 cm thick. It may have had head-butting contests to see who should be leader of the herd.

The smallest dinosaurs

We usually think of dinosaurs as huge monsters but there were some that were only the

The smallest dinosaur skeleton ever found belonged to a baby **Psittacosaurus**. It was only 23 cm long.

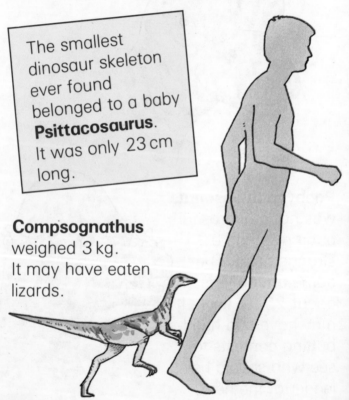

Compsognathus weighed 3 kg. It may have eaten lizards.

size of a hen or duck. These were light and quick. They could pounce on small prey or run away into the undergrowth or into a crack in the rocks to escape from their enemies.

Lesothosaurus was 90 cm long and ran on its long, thin back legs. It had a horny "beak" and probably fed on leaves and shoots.

Saltopus was a slim and speedy little meat-eating dinosaur. It was 90 cm long and weighed only about 1 kg. It probably ate insects.

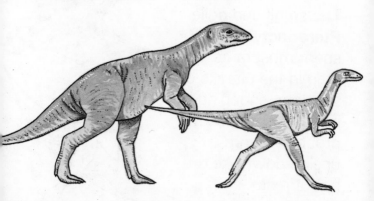

Pteranodon had a long toothless beak which it used to snatch fish from the sea. It stored them in a pouch under its beak.

The small and agile **Pterodactylus** spent most of its time in the air, like a swallow, snapping insects as it flew. It probably hung upside down like a bat at rest.

The largest animal ever to fly was **Quetzalcoatlus** with a wingspan of 12 m. It was the size of a two-seater aircraft.

Flying reptiles

Dinosaurs could not fly, but some reptiles, called *pterosaurs*, could. They ruled the skies for almost as long as the dinosaurs ruled the land. Pterosaurs were more like bats than birds. Their wings were made of leathery skin stretched between their long arms and back legs.

Sea reptiles

Throughout the age of the dinosaurs the oceans were filled with reptiles. Some looked like sea serpents with long snake-like necks, which reared out of the water. Others looked like crocodiles or dolphins. They all breathed air and came to the water's surface to breathe.

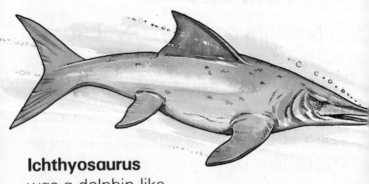

Ichthyosaurus
was a dolphin-like
reptile with a tail
like a fish and flippers. It hunted in packs
and ate squid and fish.

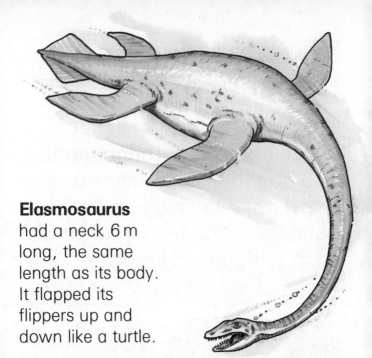

Elasmosaurus
had a neck 6 m
long, the same
length as its body.
It flapped its
flippers up and
down like a turtle.

Metriorhynchus was a fish-like
crocodile. It had a tail flipper, webbed
hands and feet and very sharp teeth.

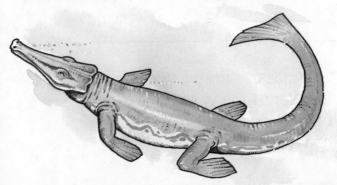

The most famous dinosaur of all

The most terrible of all the dinosaurs was **Tyrannosaurus**. The poor duckbilled dinosaur stood no chance against the huge jaws and tearing teeth of such a frightening monster.

Its jaws were 1.5 m long with huge 15 cm saw-like teeth. It tore off lumps of flesh and swallowed them whole.

The massive tail was used to balance the weight of its body and heavy head.

Tyrannosaurus was the largest known meat-eating animal ever to live on land. It was 5 m tall, 14 m long and weighed 7 tonnes.

It walked on its powerful back legs, moving at about 4 km an hour, the same speed as a human. No one knows how it used its tiny two-clawed hands.

The end of the dinosaurs

About 65 million years ago the dinosaurs and all their large reptile relatives died within a short space of time. No one knows why this happened but there are some different ideas.

Towards the end of the age of the dinosaurs many small mammals lived on Earth. Could they have stolen and eaten too many dinosaur eggs?

Perhaps Earth was struck by a huge meteorite. Dust thrown up might have blotted out the sun so that no plants could grow. Many animals would have starved to death.

Over thousands of years Earth had become colder. The huge reptiles had no fur or feathers to keep them warm. They would have frozen to death.

A story in stone

If there are no dinosaurs alive today how do we know so much about them? We know because we have found their bones, claws, teeth, eggs and footprints which over millions of years have hardened into rock. They have become fossils. Fossils are found when the rock splits or if it is worn away by wind and rain.

Not only bones become fossilised. These dinosaur footprints were made long ago in soft ground which later hardened into rock.

When this dinosaur died it fell to the bottom of a lake. All the soft parts of its body rotted away. Only its skeleton was left.

Over many years, layers of mud covered the bones. The lower layers slowly hardened into rock.

The bones themselves changed into a hard rocky material. They became fossilised.

Finding dinosaurs

Sometimes fossilised bones are found lying on the ground. Usually they are still buried, with one or two bones sticking out of the side of a cliff or quarry. The place where the bones are found is called a dig. Scientists carefully remove the bones and take them away to be rebuilt into a dinosaur.

The fossil hunter chips away at the rock around the bone. Then he uses small chisels and brushes to clear away the rest of the rock.

Some bones are weak and crumbly. They are covered with plaster-soaked bandages which harden as they dry. These protect the bones so that they can be taken away.

Before each bone is removed it is photographed and labelled so that the bones can be put in the right order when the dinosaur is rebuilt.

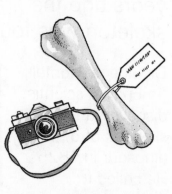

Assembling a dinosaur is like doing a huge jigsaw puzzle. It often takes months or even years to do.

Dinosaur detectives

The first dinosaur bone was discovered over three hundred years ago. The man who found it thought it came from a giant! Over one hundred and fifty years ago the first dinosaur skeleton was found.

Dr Gideon Mantell, an English scientist, discovered the skeleton of a dinosaur in 1825. He called it **Iguanodon** because he thought it looked like a giant iguana.

Othniel Marsh, who lived one hundred years ago, was a famous dinosaur detective who made many finds in North America.

"Fossil hunts" were very popular a hundred years ago. This old newspaper picture shows one such dig in the Rocky Mountains, USA in 1878.

Latest discoveries

New dinosaur fossils are being discovered all the time. Two more were found in the Gobi Desert in 1987. Each new find gives scientists a better idea of what life was like on Earth all those millions of years ago.

Ultrasaurus was an enormous plant-eating dinosaur. Its skeleton was found in 1979. Scientists think that it was taller than a five-storey building.

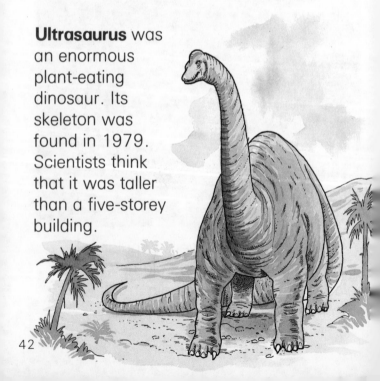

In 1983 William Walker, an English fossil hunter, found a huge claw in a Surrey quarry. Three van loads of bones were taken away to be rebuilt into a huge dinosaur which was nicknamed ''Claws''.

''Claws'' was a new species of meat-eating dinosaur. It was later named **Baryonyx walkeri**. Its famous claw was 30 cm long. It may have been used to hook fish out of the water.

Glossary of some dinosaur names in this book

Baryonyx walkeri
barri-on-iks war-ker-ry
(heavy claw)

Brachiosaurus
bra-kee-o-sor-uss
(arm reptile)

Coelophysis
see-lo-fy-siss
(hollow face)

Compsognathus
komp-sog-nay-thuss
(pretty jaw)

Deinonychus
dy-no-ny-kuss
(terrible claw)

Diplodocus
dip-plod-o-kuss
(double beam)

Euoplocephalus
u-o-plo-keff-al-uss
(true plated head)

Heterodontosaurus
het-ter-o-don-toe-sor-uss
(mixed-tooth reptile)

Iguanodon
ig-wan-o-don
(iguana tooth)

Lesothosaurus
less-o-toe-sor-uss
(reptile from Lesotho)

Mamenchisaurus
ma-men-chee-sor-uss
(reptile from China)

Megalosaurus
meg-a-loss-a-russ
(giant reptile)

Pachycephalosaurus
pak-ee-keff-al-o-sor-uss
(thick-headed reptile)

Paleoscincus
pay-lee-o-skin-kuss
(ancient skink)

Parasaurolophus
pa-ra-sor-rollo-fuss
(reptile with a parallel-sided crest)

Polacanthus
poll-a-kan-thuss
(many spined)

Protoceratops
pro-toe-sair-a-tops
(first horned face)

Psittacosaurus
si-ta-co-sor-uss
(parrot reptile)

Saltopus
sol-toe-puss
(leaping foot)

Stegosaurus
steg-o-sor-russ
(roofed reptile)

Triceratops
try-ser-a-tops
(three-horned face)

Tsintaosaurus
sin-toe-sor-uss
(reptile from Tsintao)

Tyrannosaurus
ty-ran-no-sor-uss
(tyrant reptile)

Ultrasaurus
ull-tra-sor-uss
(largest reptile)